Done Right

A SPICY NOVELLA

RHIANNA BURWELL

Chapter One

Emma

I've had my share of bad sex. People love to pretend that sex is always amazing, that you always cum six times from the dude's seventeen-inch cock, and then you can't walk after because it was just that good. I've had that kind of sex, don't get me wrong, but nothing stands out in my memory more than the bad times.

Like right now, for instance, as Joey Jacobowitz jack- hammers into me, all I can think about is how I am going to remember this piss-poor sex for the rest of my fucking life. It's not that it is horrible, it's that there is nothing going on other than the jackhammering. My clit hasn't been touched once the entire time I have been naked, and that's a big fucking red flag for me.

"Holy shit, baby," Joey whispers in my ear, spitting just a little bit. His lack of control over his saliva grosses me out, on top of the ick from being called baby by someone I barely know. I am not his baby. I just need a good lay, and honestly, he is not delivering. His cock continues thrusting into me, leaving small sensations of pleasure in its path. It's not horrible, and it still feels okay, but I have ten miles to go until I'm going to orgasm, and he is only moving an inch a minute at this rate.

If I were less seasoned, less mature, I might let him finish. I used to believe that if I am already here, I might as well finish what I started. I might as well let them have a good time, even if they won't do the same for me. But, at the ripe age of twenty-four, I am finally realizing that men deserve no such thing, and I decide I'm done with this shitty experience. I don't need to be a sex doll for this man any longer than I already have been.

"Okay, dude, I'm done," I mutter, pushing his chest until he is in an upright position. Joey sends me a shocked look before removing his cock from me.

"What?" he asks, still confused.

I lift my body from the bed, looking around for the clothes we threw on the ground when we were in a rush to get naked. I miss who I was twelve minutes ago, she was so full of hope.

"I'm done," I say again, finally finding my bra. I quickly clasp it behind me, taking away the view of my tits from Joey. He honestly doesn't deserve it.

Joey's bedroom should have been my first indication that this wasn't a love connection. The mattress sitting on the floor is adequate enough to be called a bed for him, the white sheets haven't been white in years if you ask me, and the posters, held up with push-pins, of *Sports Illustrated* models hanging on his wall, prove that he regularly stares at women as if they are objects for him to consume. Yet, I still held out hope that he could at least fuck me the way I need to be fucked, but I was let down once again.

"We just started," he says with a smirk on his face. If he thinks he can weasel his way back into my pants, he is dead wrong. I know what sex with him is like now, and I am not making that mistake twice.

"Well, I'm still done," I say for the third time, this time with more force. I don't know what it is with men who suck at fucking, never being able to take no for an answer. Either get good or get out, buddy.

"Are you fucking serious?" he says, starting to get mad. I shrug my shoulders, avoiding eye contact completely, and gasp as I finally find my shirt. I yank it on, knowing this situation is only going to escalate and I don't want to be here when it does.

I don't reply to his comment, the answer clearly obvious to me, but when I glance up at him, in the middle of trying to find my pants, his eyebrows are raised as if he is expecting an answer from me. I huff out a sigh, searching on the other side of the bed for the leggings I had on before this disaster.

"I'm not going to cum, Joey. It doesn't really seem worth it to me," I say, shrugging my shoulders. I hold eye contact with him so he knows I'm serious. Someone needs to tell him that he isn't very giving in bed, and that someone can be me. I don't really care.

I know there is value to sex besides just orgasming. I have had amazing sex where I didn't orgasm at all, but those times were different. Those times were amazing because of the connection between us, and I have no connection with Joey. I have known him for a little while. He snagged my number at the restaurant where I waitress. I thought he would be a good lay. He's quite a charmer when he has his clothes on, so I thought he could impress me with them off too.

"Are you fucking kidding me?" he says, his anger dissipating as disappointment takes over. Maybe he realized that this is more his fault than mine. Maybe he realized he should have at least *attempted* to locate my clit. Maybe he realized it really doesn't fucking matter what went wrong. I'm already half-dressed, and I am not going to get undressed again.

I finally locate my pants, which are under his own on his side of the bed. I have yet to find my underwear, but at this point, I would like to get the fuck out of here before he questions me again. I hike my pants up my legs with little regard to Joey glancing at me with shock still on his face.

"Just a little pro tip, find the clit next time," I say, before finally turning around and heading through his bedroom door. I make a beeline for his front door before I can hear his reply to my comment.

Finally outside, I start walking in the direction of Hank's Diner and Bar, hoping to be able to sit for a drink before I need to catch a ride home. Thankfully, Joey only lives about fifteen minutes away from my work. I think that was the only perk of this disappointment of a hook-up.

Chapter Two

Finn

My eyes won't stop moving to the fucking gorgeous woman sitting at the bar, and I need to get my shit together. I glance back at my date, who has not stopped talking since we got here. I said I was going to put myself out there again, and this is me really fucking trying.

There is nothing wrong with my date. Her hair is a pretty blonde that I could imagine fisting in my hand, and her pink lips would look amazing wrapped around my cock. The problem is, I've been here before. It feels like I'm not moving forward in my life anymore. I fuck the same kind of girl every Friday night, and then go to work every Monday morning with a hard cock. I never feel satisfied.

The redhead across the restaurant though, god, she could fucking satisfy me. Her red hair keeps catching my eye, making me glance over there more than I would like. Her head tips back with a laugh and the sound, even from far away, consumes my entire body. She's talking to the bartender as if they are friends, and I shake my head, trying to return to reality.

My eyes finally find Claire's again. She hasn't stopped talking since I started dazing off, and I don't blame her. I'm probably horrible company right now.

"Right?" she asks, blue eyes hopeful. She stares at me, waiting for my answer. I wish I knew what she was talking about, but I haven't been listening to a single thing she has said.

"I'm sorry?" I ask, hopefully not sounding like a jack-ass. I don't want to be rude to her, but if I'm being honest, I don't even care what we are talking about. I'm sure she would be a perfect person for someone else, but tonight, she isn't holding my interest at all. Maybe that makes me a dick, but I can't help staring at the redhead at the bar. Something about her has gotten my attention in a way no one else has.

"I said that it would be good if we went to the Carlson event together, right?" she asks again, eyes filling with hope once more. I refrain a groan from leaking out of my mouth. My PR team is hosting an event in a few weeks, mostly to raise money so rich people can continue looking like the idols they aren't. These are the kinds of events I'm supposed to bring a date to. Usually, I find a date a few weeks in advance to keep up the illusion that my life is a fucking gold mine.

Everyone expects that, because I'm big on social media and have enough money to buy anything my heart desires, I must be the happiest fucking guy alive, but I'm not. This life gets boring. It's the same thing over and over and over again, and after a while, I can't keep doing the same thing. I post the same pictures. I buy the same shit. I go out with the exact same women.

Something about the women across the restaurant though, feels different. She doesn't give off the same energy everyone else around me does. She doesn't seem like someone desperate for fame, like the rest of the people in my life. I glance over at her again, wishing she would look at me so I could see what color eyes she has.

"Uh—" I stutter, realizing I never answered Claire. Part of me wants to lie and tell her that it would be amazing to go with her to the Carlson event. Keeping up this facade would be easier than tearing it down, but part of me wants to challenge the world around me. Everyone expects me to date a supermodel who is from the same world that I am, but maybe I need to tell everyone to fuck off. Maybe, just this once, I should have a say in who I spend my time with.

"I don't think so," I finally answer, hesitating slightly. It feels unfamiliar coming out of my mouth. This is outside of the normal that has been surrounding my life for years, but at this point, I don't know if I care. I'm sick of doing the exact same things all of the time. I need something different.

"What do you mean?" Claire asks, confused. I shuffle through my thoughts for a second, hoping to find something concrete. I don't have any reason to dislike her, I just do. I need someone new and different, and I've been down this road a million times.

"I just don't think we should go together," I say, taking my wallet out of my pocket, finally done with this conversation. I was letting it go on longer than I wanted it to because that is what I do. I have been doing the easy thing for years. Going out with women who don't challenge me. Doing work that doesn't drive me. My entire life has been put on easy mode since I started on social media, and I'm sick of it.

I smack a couple of bills onto the table, leaving a hefty tip. I rise from my seat and Claire's eyes widen with shock. She stares up at me, totally confused.

"What the fuck is going on here, Finn?" she asks, panic rising in her voice.

"I think this date should be over," I state. "I had a good time and you are a wonderful person, but not the person for me," I say as gracefully as I can. The problem is not her, it's me. I shouldn't have agreed to this date in the first place. I can feel the pressures of my life starting to weigh down on me, but I've been pushing it away for weeks, hoping the feeling would go away. Instead of continuing to push it away, I'm going to embrace it.

I turn around, not in the mood to look back anymore, and walk my way across the restaurant. I shouldn't come from the table with Claire straight to the bar, but I can't help myself. The idea of trying something new tonight fills me with a fire I didn't know I needed. I thought my life had everything, but now I'm not so sure.

I find the redhead through a small sea of people. On my way over, for a moment, I lost sight of her. She isn't looking at me. Instead, she is still talking to the bartender, making my blood run hot.

I shouldn't be this interested in a stranger, but I can't help myself. My body pulls toward her, hoping to get even a fraction of an inch closer. She has the room by the throat, forcing everyone to look her way. At least, she has me by the throat. I can't stop staring at her.

I thank the universe when the seat next to her opens up as I arrive. I scoot into it quickly, feeling the heat from her skin crash into mine, making me feel warm. She glances my way, making my cock harden. I don't usually have such a reaction from a look, but she seems to influence me like no other.

For a second, just a second, my confidence wavers. I don't know what the right approach is with her. I don't want to do this the wrong way and lose a chance with her. I'm used to the same kind of woman, and I know how to pick them up. This is uncharted territory for me, and it's thrilling as much as it is terrifying.

My thoughts run dry when her voice carries itself across to me, making my body stiffen.

"Listen," she says to the bartender, slurring just a little. "I'm just sick of these men walking around like they got something good in their pants, and then disappointing me every chance they get," she says, eyes filled with humor as the bartender laughs with her. He shakes a tumbler while listening to her, before finally pouring the drink into a glass and walking it down to someone at the end of the bar.

My sight is caught by Claire exiting the building. I watch as she walks out the glass doors with her head down and for a moment, I feel bad. She doesn't deserve this. She isn't a bad person, she just isn't my person.

I take a moment to glance at the firecracker sitting next to me, fully taking her in. The outfit she is wearing could bring me to my fucking knees. I mean that literally. Her shirt is black, complimenting her hair nicely, but low cut enough to make me have to resist staring at her chest. The shirt hugs her curves, making me salivate. I try my best to seem unaffected, but this is one of the most beautiful women I have ever seen in my life.

Her brown eyes meet mine, unexpectedly, and my breath leaves my body. The colors dance in her gaze, drawing me in and forcing me to give her all of my attention.

She has her elbow on top of the bar, from previously talking with her hands to the bartender, showing the soft curve of her side in a way that catches my attention, holding it for longer than I would like to admit. My eyes trail up and stop on the curve of her neck, making me wish I could feel her soft skin on the palm of my hand. What I would give to have my hands around her throat.

"Like you!" she exclaims, pointing at me suddenly. She has a wild look in her eyes, as if her point has been proven by my presence. I look behind me, making sure that she's talking to me. She continues staring at me as if I am the one with the wild behavior.

"Me?" I ask when she refuses to say anymore. She just sits there staring at me, waiting for me to speak.

"Yes!" she shouts, loud enough for the room to hear but not loud enough to be annoying. I rear back slightly, unsure what she is talking about. Although I should be uneasy about the way she is speaking to me, it is just turning me on. I can't get over how her hair looks when she is mad, as if it has literally caught on fire. Her face is red with annoyance, for a reason I'm still not sure of, but she looks fucking radiant. Her lips are curled into a tiny little snarl, making my cock twitch in my pants. She makes me react to her, even when she seems pissed.

"You got this sexy thing going," she says, making my eyebrows raise at the boldness of her words. "But I absolutely doubt you know how to fuck," she says, ruining the self-confidence she placed in me moments ago.

"I—I," I stumble over my words. No one has honestly ever talked to me like that. Part of it is insulting, I'm not going to lie. It doesn't feel good, but a bigger part of it was riveting. Most women around me are around for my clout. I have a lot of followers on social media and usually, that means that people treat me like a king, even though I'm not that different from them. Always having to wonder about people's intentions is exhausting, so this feels like a breath of fresh air, even if it is a little disrespectful.

"If you stutter, it means I'm right," the firecracker says smugly, before finally turning away from me. I take a second to find my bearings before replying.

I know I'm not horrible in bed. All the women who tell the world about fucking me, have never complained. Though, I've never heard any upstanding reviews either. Usually, women care more about the fact *that* they fucked me than they do about how good it was. Sometimes I think that once my cock is inside them, they have checked off the box and are ready to leave.

"What's your name?" I ask, trying to find my confidence again.

"Why?" she asks, turning to look at me again with a raised eyebrow and an uneasy expression.

"I don't usually have such intimate conversations with people when I don't even know their names," I say, hoping I sound more confident than I feel. I was looking for an in to talk to her, and this is as good as any. Especially after she said the word "fuck" and it made my pants get tight.

"Emma," she finally states, looking me up and down, assessing me. I don't know what she finds, but it seems to satisfy something inside of her because she holds her hand out for me to shake.

I take her hand willingly, thankful for the contact. Electricity shoots through me when I touch her, going straight down my spine to my dick, and I'm suddenly wishing and praying she would fix the hard-on that has been sitting in my pants since I noticed her across the room.

"Finn," I say when she takes her hand out of my grasp. "See, you even have a sexy name," she says as if that proves her point even more.

"Does that add to the sexy thing I got going on then?" I ask flirtatiously, finally finding my footing in talking to her.

"Don't be smug," she replies with a roll of her eyes. God this woman makes me want to do things to her that they don't even make porn about. "That wasn't my point." Her words shake my confidence again. I feel like I keep yo-yo-ing with her. One second I'm making ground, the next I'm back to feeling self-conscious.

"No one has ever asked me if I know how to fuck before," I admit sheepishly, coming to terms with the fact that I may not be as good as I think. It feels like something so obvious, but I never even thought about it. It felt like these women and I had some sort of secret arrangement. They get to talk about me and I get laid. I hate to think about sex as transactional, but that's how it felt. The idea makes my stomach turn sour, knowing that I haven't even given any thought to my partner's pleasure until now.

I flag down the bartender, who has been running around like a chicken with his head cut off ever since Emma stopped talking to him. I order a whiskey, hoping it will eat away at the embarrassment that is flooding me.

"It's not really a common question," Emma states. The bartender asks if she wants anything else, and she shakes her head. "I think that's enough for me," she admits dryly.

I glance over at her, and the confidence she was sporting earlier has been replaced with something else, something I'm not sure of. She looks sad all of a sudden, almost shameful, and the energy changes in the room.

I understand the shame she is feeling. I'm feeling the same right about now. It feels like a bubble just burst around me. I thought my life was going well. I thought I was doing good in all areas of my life, but it feels like I have been sleeping. I have been sleeping through sex with these women because this is how it has been for years. I haven't had to think about performance, because people haven't cared about that. I push back the feeling of being used, not wanting to go there. I feel like I used them and they used me and it's a whole clusterfuck of emotions and uncomfortable feelings. I don't know if I want to deep-dive into that cesspool just yet.

"I'm sorry. I just had a shitty night. I'm sure you fuck just fine," she states regretfully, leaning into me when she speaks. Her arm presses against mine, only for a second, but the touch leaves my body feeling cold when she leans away.

"I don't know if I do actually," I admit. I don't want to come to terms with this, but it feels like something I need to do. I need to deal with this because what I have been doing isn't right. Everyone is fine if I use them as a sex doll, as long as they get to tell people they fucked Finn Declan. Emma looks me up and down again, searching for answers that are sitting on my tongue. I try to pull the sour look o! of my face, making my bad mood less obvious, but I can't get my muscles to cooperate. It feels like I have been sleepwalking for years, and I just woke up.

"I got popular at eighteen, and I mean *really* popular. No one cares if I fuck them good, as long as they can sell the story to the gossip magazine the next day," I say with a shrug of my shoulders, trying to explain the best I can. I sound sadder than I intended and I do my best to put the mask back on. I'm supposed to be happy. I have everything the world has to offer me, but I haven't been happy in years. My life doesn't even feel like my own anymore and it's taken me this long to see that something isn't right.

"That's fucking sad," Emma says, pulling me from my thoughts. I glance at her, and her eyes hold sympathy. I have been pushing away these feelings for years because I wasn't sure if I even deserved sympathy. I didn't think someone could ever feel bad for the rich guy with too much pussy, but Emma looks at me like my problems are real. Like what I am going through matters, and that has never happened before.

"It is what it is," I say, downing my whiskey and staring at the table. I don't give myself many moments to feel bad for myself, so I take this moment and I stew in it, because tomorrow, it will be back to PR meetings and fake smiles.

I search for some way out of this conversation. It feels too big right now. I need to focus back on her and move this into something lighter. Something that doesn't make me feel like a failure of a man for the last twenty-six years.

"What's your story then? What's got you asking questions like that?" I mutter, hoping she will take the bait and turn the conversation back on her, but she doesn't answer right away. She thinks hard, moving her mouth from side to side, as if chewing on the words before she opens up to me. "You have bad sex or something?" I finally ask. There has got to be a story there. Normal people don't sit in bars tipsy, telling strangers they can't fuck well.

"Oh my god, is it that obvious?" she asks, looking exhausted over the topic. "I fucked a dude legit twenty minutes ago, and I don't even think he knew what a clit was," she says, and I wince at her words. It feels like too much information and not enough at the exact same time.

"Hey, at least I know what a clit is," I say, raising my glass in a toast.

"I hate to break it to you, but that doesn't mean you are good with it," she says, rolling her eyes. The smile on her face gives it away though. She might be warming up to me.

"Touché," I say, laughing, allowing silence to take over the conversation for a second. The longer we talk, the faster my hope of taking this woman home plummets.

Starting the conversation by admitting that I may not know how to fuck might not have been my best strategy.

"Wait, you're Finn Declan?" Emma asks, finally making the connection with wide eyes and an open mouth in the shape of an "O." "Oh my god, of course you fucking are!" she exclaims, putting her hand on my arm as the connection registers on her face. I can feel her heat through my shirt and it lights me up inside. I stare at her mouth for a few beats too long, but I can't stop imagining sliding my cock inside of those pretty lips. I push my dirty thoughts away, trying to get a handle on myself. I've never felt so out of control over my thoughts, but Emma brings something new out of me. "I can't believe I didn't see it before." She removes her hand from my arm, shaking her head while the heat leaves my body, once again leaving me feeling cold. This is usually the moment when someone asks for my autograph, if I will follow them on Instagram, or some other bullshit that I don't want to do. I don't mean to sound cocky, but it has happened so many times that I have come to expect it at this point.

"You're like a billionaire, aren't you?" she asks, looking at me again with a new expression I can't register. Her stare feels hot on my skin, but her question cools me back down instantly. Bingo. This is where she offers to fuck me because of who I am. I should have kept my mouth shut.

"More or less," I say vaguely, hoping she doesn't start screaming it for the whole restaurant. It wouldn't be the first time that has happened and it probably won't be the last.

The scoff that comes out of her mouth surprises me. "What does that mean?" I ask, suddenly intrigued by her answer. This is not what usually happens to me. No one has ever disliked the amount of money sitting in my bank account. Usually, it is more of a reason to get me into bed.

"Nothing," she says, a small smirk playing on her lips. She raises a glass of water to her lips, compliments of the bartender who keeps glancing over here to make sure she is okay. I appreciate him checking in, but it makes me curious to know who he is to her.

"What was that sound for then?" I ask, humor playing in my voice. I'm mostly joking, it shouldn't matter what this stranger at a bar thinks about my life choices, but a teeny-tiny part of me is desperate to hear someone be fucking truthful for once in their lives. I have an insane lifestyle, being this level of celebrity. I love it, don't get me wrong, but after years, I'm exhausted with trying to figure out who is telling the truth and who is lying straight to my face.

"I just mean—" she stops, shaking her head as if there is a war waging in there. I raise my eyebrows at her, hoping to finally get a response. "Eat the rich, ya know?" she says finally, shrugging as she takes another drink with a smile on her face. She says this as if the phrase means anything to me. Confusion seeps into my body, not knowing what the fuck she is talking about.

"Is that a sex thing?" I ask. She laughs at my comment, making me even more confused than I was before.

"No, it's like—" she stops, moving her arms in a way that makes me believe she doesn't quite know how to phrase it. "It's just the idea that there shouldn't be billionaires. You are sucking all the wealth out of the economy," she says, laughing at my shocked face.

"So your phrase for that... is eat the rich?"

"Yeah," she says matter-of-factly as if that makes all the sense in the world. I open my mouth to speak and close it, then do it all over again. Confusion seeps into my pores. Most people in my position, might get mad that they aren't getting treated with the respect celebrities are used to, but I have been so desperate for someone to just be fucking honest that this is more refreshing than anything. I don't even want to admit how much this is turning me on. Finally finding a woman who doesn't fall at my feet feels like the thing my life has been missing for years.

"I have never met someone who is *mad* about my wealth," I say, absolutely shocked even after moments to process what she said.

"I mean, I'm not *mad* about it," she explains, her red hair moving with her as she talks. Her hair makes me think of fire because if I get too close to her, I could get fucking burned. The attraction that I feel for her, already, is unparalleled to anything I have felt before. "I just probably don't want to fuck you now," she says, with a shrug and a smirk.

"Oh, so you wanted to fuck me before, then?" I ask with a laugh, shocked and excited at her confession. She laughs at my words, sending chills down my spine. I'm relishing the reaction this woman gets out of me. I have never felt like this before.

"Like you said," Emma mutters as she bats her eyelashes at me. "You don't even think you are any good," she says with mock innocence. Her lips get extra pouty when she talks like that and I feel my cock stir in my pants. It wants nothing more than to feel her lips around it, but it seems like the chances of that happening are slipping further and further out of my grasp.

"I mean, you'll never know unless you find out," I say, wishing she would take me up on the offer. She turns in her seat, facing me fully. She assesses me with her eyes, making me hungry for her. I watch as her eyes trail my body, leaving !re in their path. I do the same thing, taking in her whole body with my eyes, wishing I could do a lot more than just stare at her.

"I don't usually get into bed with someone with the intention of being disappointed," she says, voice hoarser than before, making me think that she's turned on. That I'm turning her on. I don't know much about women, but I know when they want to fuck. I smirk, knowing I have an influence on her, even if it is only half of the influence she has on me.

"I'm a very quick learner," I say, placing my hand on her knee, which is only a few inches away from me since she turned her body. Her breath hitches and that gives me the go-ahead to move my hand, only slightly at first. I trail my fingers up her leg with the lightest touch I can muster, only an inch or two every second, giving her time to stop me if she wants. Giving her time to tell me this is a bad idea. She should tell me that I am playing with fire, but she doesn't. Her eyes hold the fire inside of them, contained only for now.

Chapter Three

Emma

I stare into his eyes, hoping the answer to the questions swarming my head, will be made clear. The alcohol is wearing off, making my rationale come back to me. I'm no longer the drunk girl in the bar yelling at men about how they can't fuck. Now I'm the sober girl at the bar, wanting to fuck said man.

He's fucking gorgeous, honestly. The way his shirt is clinging to his body makes me sweat, it's so sexy. He commands the room with force, making everyone aware of his presence, even if they don't recognize him. His brown eyes stare back at me like I am the sun, moon, and stars. No one has ever looked at me like that. I feel like he would fall at my feet if I asked him to, and he would thank me for the opportunity.

His body is to die for, with strong arms that I have a hard time keeping my eyes off of, eyes that I could drown in, and a presence that leaves me breathless. He is dressed beautifully, in a crisp white button-up shirt and a pair of fancy-looking dress pants. His looks scream money, and that makes sense. He has more money than I could ever dream of having, only instead of that being a good thing, I place it in the con column of the pros and cons chart in my head.

The thing that I keep coming back to, though, is his openness. Men, in general, never want to admit they don't know how to fuck. If I had talked to any other man in the bar tonight, they would have instantly bragged about how they would "rock my world" if given the opportunity, and guess what? They'd disappoint me, every time. Usually, the men who need to tell you they are good in bed, are not actually as good as they think.

Instead of Finn trying to convince me he could kill me with orgasms, he was just honest. Something about that makes me want him even more than I did before. Something about his openness and vulnerability makes me want to do the same. Something about it makes me want to give him a chance.

I don't know how to explain what is happening inside of my body. A huge sense of power rushes through me all at once and

I feel like I can do anything I want to. I feel so in control of the situation. I feel free to do whatever the fuck my heart and pussy want, and let me fucking tell you, they want Finn.

Finn takes a sip of his second drink, the whiskey he got a few minutes ago from Ash, the bartender. Finn and I stare at each other for a few beats, sitting in the sexual energy. I can still feel where his hand traced my leg a few minutes ago, before he removed it when Ash walked up to ask if we needed anything else. I think I saw a hint of jealousy wash over his face, but it was so quick, I can't be sure. "So you'd just like... take direction from me?" I say, with an innocent voice, while sliding my hand onto his thigh, trying to give him the same feelings he gave me. His breath hitches at my words, and his eyes dart down to his leg, staring at my hand as I run my fingers over his pants.

I can't believe I'm doing this. I can't believe I am considering this. Finn Declan is not only incredibly famous, but he has more money than I can even imagine. He is so out of my league, yet he still sits there looking like I am the hottest thing he has ever seen. The feeling gets me drunk, making me bold.

"I could try," he says, voice hoarse. His eyes stay trained on his leg, never leaving to look up at my face. I move my hands a few inches closer to his cock. I can't see the outline through his pants, they aren't quite tight enough, but I know he is hard, based on the way he is talking to me and the desire burning in his eyes.

"I just want—" he mumbles, stumbling on his words. I bat my eyelashes at him, waiting for him to speak. I need him to confirm that he wants this. That he wants me to take the lead here. I need to know if I'm alone in this, or if this is gonna be the best night of my fucking life.

"I just want it to be good for you," he says, looking down at my hand on his thigh again. This man interests me. I don't know if he knows what it's like to *know* when a woman is enjoying herself. It's so bizarre to me because that's the point of sex in my opinion. If I want just orgasms, I have a battery-operated toy that will do the job just fine. I go into sex for the intimacy and the chance to watch someone else fall apart. I don't know if he has ever even experienced that.

"Have you ever felt someone cum on your cock?" I whisper, leaning closer to him than needed. My voice is hoarser than I intended, but I'm hoping it comes off sexy, instead of making me sound like a chain smoker. His breath hitches again when my words hit his ears, and he readjusts in his seat, clearly getting turned on.

"I don't know," he says, looking me in the eyes with a desperation I have never seen from a man before. The eye contact makes my nipples peak inside my shirt. I wish we were in a place where he could touch me. Fuck, I just want this man to touch me.

"Oh, you'd know," I say, because he would. If you have to question if a woman came or not, then she didn't. If you don't know if you have ever felt it, then you never have, and that's a damn fucking shame. A man with a body like Finn's should know how to use it.

"How?" he asks, baiting me. I smile at him, more turned on than he knows. He sits there like he doesn't have much game. Like women literally fall into his lap without him uttering a word, but he is making me wet just with his curiosity. He should try this more often, maybe he would have people cumming left and right.

"You can feel it on your cock," I say, running my finger over the crotch of his pants. It's rock hard under his clothes, and it takes everything inside of me not to tell him to take me to the bathroom already.

I'm enjoying this build-up more than I would care to admit though.

He clears his throat, unable to get words out for a second. I feel my body react to that sound more than it reacted to Joey sticking his cock inside of me. I want to make love to that fucking sound. I want to marry that fucking sound. I want to spread that sound over a piece of toast and eat it for days.

"You can feel it?" he finally asks, once he gets a handle on his voice. My eyes scan down his face, taking rest stops at every area. His eyes hold my attention for ages. The brown mixing with gold, making me feel seen. His mouth is pouty in the perfect fucking way. His facial hair makes my mouth fucking water.

He looks fucking hungry, but not for something he could eat. He looks hungry with desire and knowing it is directed at me makes me literally soak through my panties. "Whenever I cum at least," I say slowly, trailing the words off to make him desperate. His tongue pops out, wetting his bottom lip and I hold back a whimper that threatens to escape. I have never been so turned on by something so simple. "I usually get tighter when I cum," I state simply, leaving so much information up in the air.

I love this game we are playing. I give him tiny pieces, always leaving him desperate for me to tell him more. I have never felt like this. I have never felt like I had the keys to someone's body so easily. I have never had this much influence over someone.

"You get tighter?" he whispers, meaning no one else in the room can hear him other than me. Not that there are many people in the room at this point. His voice sounds so fucking desperate. Like he is hanging on to my every fucking word.

"A lot tighter," I whisper in his ear, finally bringing my hand fully up to his cock. I swear I can feel it throb in my hand, even through his pants, but I don't leave my hand there long enough to know for sure.

"You want to get out of here?" he asks, finally. He looks like he is in pain, and maybe he is. I'm sure having a dick that hard would get painful after a while, and my shameless flirting has not helped.

"I thought you'd never ask," I say, standing up and grabbing my stuff, more ready than ever to fuck a stranger.

Chapter Four

Finn

I never believed in love at first sight, but I know for a fact that lust at first sight is fucking real. I've been tiptoed around for years by people who haven't interested me. I mean sure, everyone was good-looking, but their intentions were clear. I got laid, and they got the attention they wanted. They got to tell people they fucked Finn Declan, and I got to fuck. It was a perfect win-win situation.

I wasn't aware though, that giving pleasure could be as good as getting it, if not better.

The idea of *feeling* someone come apart on my dick? It feels like a fucking shame I haven't gotten to experience that, honestly. I thought I was getting the most out of these situations, but I think I may have been missing the entire fucking point.

Emma is holding my hand, dragging me across the city. The warm air feels good on my skin, but I barely even notice, because I can't stop glancing at Emma as she walks in front of me. I don't know exactly where we are headed, and maybe I should be paying more attention, but my eyes keep running down her body, completely transfixed. The sounds of horns honking and people talking glide past my ears. I know it's happening but I don't fully process it with the chatter inside my head.

I've been around the best of the best when it comes to beautiful women. At least, what society will tell you is the best of the best, but none of them have the raw sex appeal that Emma has. Maybe it's because I've never heard a woman talk to me like that. I've never heard someone sound so innocent when talking about something so primal.

Although I'm ready to open my eyes to the other side, part of this is fucking intense. There's a lot of pressure on me to perform and I need to learn what the fuck I'm doing before I let another woman down in the bedroom. Thankfully I have someone who is going to teach me.

Images of Emma being my sexy teacher in a mini skirt flood my brain, making my cock pulse in my pants. I don't think it has gone soft since she first touched my thigh at the bar.

We suddenly turn a corner, facing a bunch of small apartments. The building is probably about ten stories tall with about fifteen apartments on each level. It looks tight and crowded, but maybe that's just because tightness is on my mind.

It's like my brain has completely switched off since she said that. It feels like such a primitive need to feel her cum while wrapped around my cock.

I can't believe I have gone this long without experiencing it, but it ends today.

I follow her into the apartment, which is nothing special. It's a big building with hundreds of hallways and doors leading into places I couldn't care less about. Emma starts making her way up the stairs, and I follow like a puppy dog. Maybe I should be embarrassed about how willing I am to follow her wherever she goes, but my brain is too filled with dirty thoughts to think about anything else.

We finally reach the second floor, and she opens a door, which I assume leads into her place, and I follow her willingly.

Once we are inside, with the door closed, I give myself a moment to take a deep breath and take in her apartment. The walls are mostly bare, except for a few choice pieces of art that I don't get a good look at. It's mostly an open space with the front door opening to the living room and kitchen combined. My eyes trail back to hers and the reality of the situation hits me. Everything is moving so quickly, and I'm fucking happy about it. I feel like I can't wait another moment until I'm inside of her, but fuck this feels like a life-changing moment.

"Take your pants off," she whispers, breaking the silence, and I comply instantly. I bring my hands down to the button of my jeans, undoing it quickly. I slide my pants down my thighs, leaving me in just my underwear. My cock pulses with anticipation, desperate for Emma to touch it.

I have certain expectations about tonight already. Maybe I should have left them at the door, but images of Emma cumming on my face and cock won't leave my mind. But I wasn't expecting Emma to fall to her knees in front of me once my pants came off. She continues to stare at me the whole time, even as she lowers herself. Her gaze goes straight to my dick, making me desperate for her to touch me in some way. She stares up at me for a few seconds, waiting... for what? I don't know.

"I'm worried you're going to cum too quick," she says, holding eye contact with me still. Her words don't register for a second, I'm still too lost in my own fantasies.

"I probably will," I admit sheepishly when I finally process what she said. I wish it wasn't the truth, but with the way she is looking at me right now, I'm not going to last very long. I'm worried I'm going to cum without her even touching me. I can't imagine how I will feel with her lips wrapped around my cock.

"If I make you cum first, can you get hard again?" she asks, and before I even hear the entire sentence, my head is nodding in agreement. All I can think about right now is Emma sucking the cum out of my dick. I rip my shirt off instantly, anticipation running through my blood.

Her hands instantly go to my thighs and her gaze shifts back to the outline of my dick sitting in front of her. The way her breathing shifts, just slightly, is the biggest ego boost I have ever received in all my fucking years on this planet. She runs the tips of her fingers up and down my thighs, making me more and more desperate by the second. Even teasing me like this is getting me closer and closer to blowing a load in my boxers like a teenager.

She reaches the top of my boxers for what feels like the hundredth time and, finally, painstakingly slow, slides them down my thighs, exposing my cock to the cold air. My breath hitches in my throat. I'm right on the fucking edge, from nothing other than talking about her touching me and some light strokes on my thighs. I have never felt like this before, and I don't know how I am going to go back to mediocre hookups with women who only care about my clout.

She stares up at me again, my cock almost hitting her in the face. I don't want to brag, but my size has never been a problem in the bedroom. Lack of trying? That's been my big issue, but that changes today.

She stares at my cock, fully taking it in. She licks her lips, making me ache with lust that I haven't felt in my entire fucking life. She sticks her tongue out, grazing it against the bottom of the tip, making me dizzy. It's such a simple touch, but it makes pleasure course through my veins.

She does it again, running her tongue under the tip, forcing a moan out of my mouth before I have a chance to stop myself. She looks up at me as shock and embarrassment register in my bones. Usually, I'm not one to make noises like that, but with what she is doing, I couldn't stop myself.

"Sorry," I mumble, wishing she couldn't get those sounds out of me. Wishing this wasn't setting the standard for every other sexual encounter I will ever have. Embarrassment floods my body with how much she influences me.

"Don't apologize, just do it again," she says, voice hoarse. Her words register in my head but, before I have a chance to decipher exactly what she means, her tongue is on my cock again and I can't hold myself back. My head falls back as shocks of pleasure pulse down my spine, making my legs weak.

Instead of a simple lick this time, she keeps going. She finally takes the entire tip in her mouth, and my gaze shoots back down to her, wanting to watch my cock enter her mouth. The sight makes my cock twitch, making me nervous I won't be able to last long enough to hold onto my pride.

I'm shocked when my eyes meet hers, but the feeling doesn't even register in my head, I'm so turned on. She stares up at me while she sucks on the tip of my cock and brings me closer and closer to the orgasm I have been desperate for all night.

When she starts taking my cock deeper, I groan again and her eyes light on fire. Realization hits me that she likes it when I make noises. If I'm reading her right, she is getting turned on hearing me moan for her.

"Fuck," I mutter, watching her for a reaction. Her eyes light up again, excited about the small amounts of dirty talk coming out of my mouth. I take note of this, bookmarking it for later use, hopefully.

"Holy fuck," I mutter again, coming up short on what to say. I have never dirty-talked much. I didn't see the point. Sex to me was always quick. In and out. We both walk away happy but for completely different reasons.

She's still taking my cock deeper, but so fucking slow. Her lips start to pass about halfway, and my cock is already pulsing with need inside her mouth. I want to fill her fucking throat with cum. It feels like such a primal need, to make her take my cock.

"Yeah, fucking take it," I say, bringing my hips up a little and making my cock go deeper. Her eyes spark again, gladly taking my cock in her throat. She gets to the base of my cock, finally holding the entire thing in her throat, and her eyes stare up at me for a second. It's the sexiest fucking thing I've ever seen. Her eyes, wet with tears from adjusting to my size, stare at me, so filled with lust and desire that I can feel it just from her stare.

She bobs her head a little, shifting my cock in her throat, pushing me closer to the edge.

"I'm gonna fucking cum if you keep doing that, Emma," I say desperately. I have the urge to take her hair in my hand and take what I want, but for once I'm excited to be at someone else's mercy. She is having her filthy way with my cock, and I'm loving every second.

She takes her mouth off of my cock for only a second. "Cum in my throat," she says with pleading eyes, before resuming working my cock like a fucking professional. That's all I need. Her words send me over the edge into straight bliss. I can feel my cock pulse, emptying my load in her throat, but it feels like an out-of-body experience. It's such an intense pleasure surging through my body that I lose track of anything else other than how fucking amazing this feels.

When I finally start to come back down to earth, Emma is taking my cock out of her mouth, doing a final swallow of the cum I just released.

"Jesus Christ, Emma," I say, unable to control the reaction I'm having. I knew I loved blowjobs, but that was something else entirely. I have never gotten a blowjob like that, and I don't think I will ever be able to go back.

If I can have that kind of reaction just from her mouth, I can't even fucking imagine what she can make me feel from other parts of her body. I can't even imagine how I'm going to feel when I finally watch her come apart on my dick. The thought alone makes my cock spring back to life, ready to feel her get tight with orgasms.

Chapter Five

Emma

I've given head a hundred times. It's something that I usually enjoy, but that was something else. Holy fuck, that was something else. I'm too used to the narrative where the guy thrusts his cock into my mouth without making a sound. The guy takes pleasure from me without giving me any inclination that he is enjoying himself. Only when he finishes, do I know that he had a good time while I was on my knees.

This time, though, Finn made me feel like a fucking blowjob goddess. I wanted nothing more than to make him cum and only because I knew he would praise me with his words and noises. His moans feel like rewards that I have been granted for doing a good job, and it lights a fire inside of me that I didn't even know had been burnt out long ago.

I feel like I'm waking up a part of my body that has been asleep my entire life. I know sex can be good, but at the very least, I want it to feel equal. I want to feel the same pleasure that men are allowed to feel, and if I don't, then it isn't worth it to me to fuck someone.

This feels different. I'm not ticking boxes and hoping we get the same amount of pleasure, because his pleasure makes me so fucking hot. I didn't realize that watching Finn fall apart would make me feel more satisfaction than an hour's worth of jackhammering from a rando from the bar. I wasn't aware that I could feel this strong and powerful during sex. I didn't realize it was less about the quality of sex and more about the quality of the man.

And let me fucking tell you, Finn Declan is a fine quality man.

I finally rise from my knees, with a helping hand from Finn, and his mouth is on mine before I can even say anything.

In the past, men have been worried about kissing me after oral, especially after they cum in my mouth. It has always been a point of contention for me. I went through the trouble to suck your dick, and now I get denied a kiss because you think it's gross? Yet, when I got ready to be denied a kiss, Finn reached for me. He kisses me like he would walk through fire to feel my lips on his, and I relish the feeling.

That's a feeling I could get high on. As if he will stop at nothing to have his hands on me, and his mouth on mine. That's more powerful than any drug I have tried.

I can feel his confidence growing with his movements. When we first started, he didn't want to make many choices. He wanted me to lead the way, but I can see the more time passes, the more confident he gets in his ability to turn me on.

Probably because he has been turning me on this entire fucking time.

He pushes me against a wall, lifting me up so my legs can wrap around his torso in the most delicious way. His cock is still out, but his pants are finally all the way off, so it's just my pants stopping him from being inside of me.

He kisses me with a passion I have never known. I have been led to believe that men don't enjoy kissing the way that I do. I thought they only did it to get to the fucking faster. Yet, here I am, getting kissed like my life depends on it, and it's getting me so fucking wet I can't believe it.

Too many times I have been in a situation where someone tries to stick their dick in me, and there's a tug and a pull and a whole lot of skin pinching, all because they did nothing to prep the area other than slapping their dick across my face, which did a lot more for them than it did for me.

When Finn fucks me, we won't have that problem. He is going to slide right in with no issues. The thought makes me want to close my legs, desperate for some kind of friction. Any kind of friction at this point.

His hands are in my hair and on my ass as if he can't get quite enough of me. As if he needs to touch every part of me now or he will fucking die. I have never felt hotter. I have never thought about my appearance less. I have never had this good of a time during sex, and he hasn't even fucked me yet.

His lips leave mine and I hold back a whimper. "Where's your bedroom?" he asks, barely above a whisper. God, that voice alone could ruin my whole fucking life. I point in the direction of my room, at least I think it is the direction of my room. I can't be too sure of anything right now when my head is filled with thoughts of Finn's cock doing nasty things to my body all night.

He moves me easily with strength I haven't seen before. I wouldn't call myself a small person. I'm a normal-sized adult, but he can still carry me to my bedroom without a problem, which turns me on even more. I think everything this man can do is going to turn me on, and I just need to face that fact now.

When he lays me down on my bed, his lips join mine again, making me actually whimper this time.

"Jesus fucking Christ, make that fucking sound again," he grunts out from what I believe are gritted teeth. His tone of voice starts building pleasure at the bottom of my spine. I can't believe the way his words make my body feel fucking alive.

"Make me," I say back, humor dripping from my voice. Although I am trying to be funny, a huge huge *huge* part of me wants him to do it. I want him to make me squirm. I want him to use his body against mine in chemical goddamn warfare. I want to be at his mercy like I never have been before, like he was just at mine.

His mouth leaves mine suddenly. I stare up at him, waiting for his next move. His eyes dart between mine, looking for an answer to a question he hasn't asked yet. I wait, as patiently as I can, for him to tell me what exactly he is thinking. I want to ask him why he stopped the best experience of my fucking life.

"Can I—" he mumbles, unsure of his own words. I say nothing, trying to give him the space to ask for what he wants. I don't know if he has ever done this before, communicating to the extent that we are right now. If I'm being honest, this level of communication is new to me too. I haven't had someone be so open sexually, in my entire life. It's liberating at the same time as it is scary.

I can feel my pussy throb, desperate for him to touch me, but I continue waiting. I want to give him time to find his voice. I don't want to push. I don't want to tell him what to do. I want to give him the space to ask for what he wants, exactly how he wants it. I want him to be an active participant in this, not just someone trying to blow a load into a warm hole.

"Can I eat you out?" he finally asks, sounding like a parched man who has finally found a glass of water.

"You want to?" I ask, completely unsure. I'm not used to men being on the cusp of begging to eat my pussy. Usually, it feels more like a chore for men than anything. He nods his head instantly, reassuring me that he actually wants to do this. I nod back at him, trying to dampen the nerves that always come with receiving oral.

Although I like oral, it has always felt like something men do to check a box instead of a privilege for them. The way Finn is looking at me, with so much excitement and sexual energy, makes me feel the way I have always wanted to feel. I have always felt like giving oral is just a step right before sex, but Finn looks enthralled at the chance to eat me out.

"I've never—" he cuts off. I look him in the eyes, trying to understand exactly what he means. He can't mean he's never... gone down there? Right?

"You've never?" I ask, hoping it's not what I think it is. "I've never eaten pussy before," he says sheepishly, avoiding eye contact. I train my face to avoid showing shock. I don't want to embarrass him. "No one ever asked for it. Usually, the women I have slept with want it over quickly so they can tweet about it," he mumbles, unsure of his words.

Although the feelings flooding my body are fucking carnal, I realize now that this is incredibly vulnerable for Finn. He is doing something he hasn't done before, and he's trusting me with that. It feels like a fucking award that he would trust me with something so personal, but I dampen down the feeling, trying to focus on my reply.

"You can eat me out," I say, trying my best to sound encouraging. He gives me a hesitant look, before lifting me up far enough to take my shirt and bra off. He does so quickly, giving me zero time to care about how I look. With the top half of my body bare, Finn starts trailing kisses down my body.

Starting on my neck, he pecks, licks, and bites his way to the core of my body, leaving me in so much anticipation that I'm desperate by the time he reaches the hem of my pants. He taps my thigh, in a signal to raise my ass up, and pulls my pants off with ease and speed. Suddenly, I'm in front of him completely bare.

I hold my legs together, nerves dancing in my stomach. Usually, with a new person, nerves are present the entire time, keeping my orgasm far away, but with Finn, the nerves sit in my stomach, making the entire experience more exciting.

Finn takes in my body, running his eyes down slowly, soaking in every inch of exposed skin that I have on display. I feel the heat of his gaze, making a path down my body until it hits my legs, still closed out of either instinct or nervousness, I'm not totally sure.

"Spread your legs," he says, the most forceful he has been all night. The words slide through the room like fucking honey, making me melt into them. I want to catch those words and put them in a jar. I want to eat the words alive, letting them sustain me for weeks.

I do as I am told, spreading my legs for him to see the most personal part of my body.

I don't even think about how wet I must be. He has been using and edging my body in more ways than one for what seems like hours. The foreplay started at the bar, and it has been making me desperate for him ever since.

When his eyes rake across my open legs, his face contorts into pain, bliss, desire, and need all at once. A hundred emotions dance on his face but one stands out against the rest, complete and utter desperation for my body. The thought alone makes my orgasm start to build, and he hasn't even touched me yet. The look on his face alone will be used as spank bank material for years to come.

He moves his body to the floor, pulling me closer to the edge of the bed so he can taste me. He pulls me with force, moving me quickly. My skin slides across the bed, adding more sensations to the ever-growing desire inside of me. I feel so sensitive. Finn's touch on my ankle is incredibly soft but deliciously desperate. The soft sheets under my body ground me back to earth. The cool air hits my nipples, making them hard and desperate for someone to touch them. For Finn to touch them.

Even though I am spread in front of him, he goes impossibly slow, making me grateful and frustrated. Part of me needs a second to catch my breath. I have never had sex like this, and it is something I want to hold on to for my whole fucking life. But I'm also so fucking desperate for this man to touch me. I am so desperate to show Finn what sex *can* be, even if I am just finding out for myself.

He trails kisses up my legs, getting closer and closer to where I need him. Although I am frantic, part of me wonders if Finn needs a deep breath too. Living your entire life the way he has must make vulnerability hard. I can only imagine.

His hot breath on my thigh makes me whimper, wishing he would finally put me out of my misery.

Chapter Six

Finn

I should be nervous. I know I should be feeling some kind of anxiety, going into this. Yet, while I watch Emma get more and more frustrated with my constant teasing, my body is fucking alive. I have never felt a desire like this before. I continue kissing up her leg, finally kissing her thighs. She looks at me with so much desperation in her eyes that I almost cave. I almost skip the next few minutes and bury my face in between her legs, only coming up when I am in need of air. Only taking a breath when absolutely fucking necessary, but I want this to feel the same way for her as it does for me.

After listening to her talk at the bar, she hasn't had a good track record with men pleasing her. She seemed so frustrated that her pleasure was being put on hold for a man, and I want nothing more than to be the opposite of that. I want to put her pleasure first. I want her to think about this night for fucking years because god knows I will.

I don't know when this crossed the boundary between just fucking, and this being an emotional experience, but somewhere along the way it did. It seems so weird to trust someone this much, someone that I barely know, but I do. From the minute I sat down at the bar, I've opened myself up to Emma in a way I haven't before. Her body is completely open and bare in front of me, but this doesn't just feel like sticking my dick in someone anymore. This has advanced into something else.

I'm finally at the tops of her thighs, and I'm taking my goddamn sweet time. I have spent the most time here, sucking and biting, just a few inches away from where she wants me, where she needs me.

It may seem like nerves, but really I am just relishing this fucking woman. I have never had someone get so fucking turned on by the smallest things that I do.

Finally, fucking finally, I bring my mouth down on her pussy and her taste explodes on my tongue, making me release a moan. I run my tongue along her clit, knowing enough to know where to start, just not where to go from there.

"Yes, yes, just like that," she says, directing me on how to please her body. Instead of guessing what pleasures her, I watch her body, so fucking carefully, trying to pinpoint what feels good and what doesn't.

"Oh my god, do that again," she whimpers as I slide my tongue up and down, testing. I do it again and her moans fill the room, making my cock rock solid.

She moves her hips, directing me to where she wants me. I keep running my tongue back and forth, over the spots that make her react the most. Any time I try to move too far down, she brings my head back up with her hips, keeping me exactly where she wants me.

I slide my tongue across her clit again, making her back arch and a sound come out of her mouth that could make me cum right here. I keep doing that, watching for when it becomes too much for her. I put my whole mouth on her clit, sucking like my life depends on it. I can't believe I have gone my whole life without seeing a woman like this. Without seeing Emma like this. I'm unsure if I was really living before. Instead, I was just floating around, unaware of what I was missing.

Her back arches again when I continue working my tongue and I chance a view towards her, wondering with awe what she looks like. Her hands are on her tits, tugging and pulling on her nipples. I wish everything she did wasn't so sexy, but that sight makes my cock literally twitch between my legs. I use one hand to keep her legs spread and bring the other down on my cock, stroking it to the sight of her coming apart on my mouth.

Her words halt me. "Are you jerking off?" she asks, staring down at me with amazement in her gaze. My stomach drops a little, worried I fucked up the social etiquette of pussy eating. Maybe I am supposed to only focus on her while I do this. Maybe I am doing the same thing her exes have done, making everything about my pleasure and forgetting hers. I just couldn't keep my hands off myself. Watching her squirm on my mouth was too fucking good. I didn't even think about it, my cock just needed to be touched.

I gulp. "Yes?" I say, worried that it is the wrong answer. She swallows hard, making my gaze shift to her neck.

"You have to stop," she says, breathlessly and my stomach sinks further. I start shaking my head immediately, unsure of exactly how I have fucked this up so quickly.

"I'm sorry, I wasn't trying to ruin it," I stammer, hoping she forgets about my misstep and lets me continue making her come apart on my mouth.

"No, I—" she starts but stops and laughs instead. She looks at me with an adoration that confuses me. I thought she was pissed. "If you keep going like that, I'm going to cum," she says, pink staining her cheeks as the words leave her mouth. Realization dawns on me. It wasn't that she hated the fact that I was jerking off, she fucking likes it, a lot.

"That would make you cum?" I ask, not quite believing it.

She nods instead of answering, her cheeks staining a deeper shade of red. "You wanted me to cum on your cock, so I figured we should... stop," she says regretfully, like this was a hard choice for her to make. Blood rushes to my dick for the hundredth time tonight, hearing those words come out of her mouth.

"The only thing better than feeling you cum on my cock, is feeling you cum on my face," I say, with the most confidence I have had all night. I lower my mouth back down on her clit, slowly in case she wants to stop me. Her head falls back instantly, moans leaking out of her mouth seemingly beyond her control.

This time I don't stop. I don't go slow. I don't make her beg for it. I move my tongue in the exact way she has been desperate for until she is grinding her clit on my face. I can feel how desperate she is for release. This goes on a few more seconds, before her hands come down on my hair, pushing me onto her with force. I eat it up honestly. I love watching her get more and more desperate as time goes on.

Finally, fucking finally, she moans louder, gasping for air, letting me know she is cumming. Her back arches off the bed and her sounds light up the fucking room. I want nothing less than to have this moment last forever, but she comes down eventually, breathing heavily.

Chapter Seven

Emma

"Holy fucking shit," I mutter, coming down from one of the best orgasms of my life. I sit firmly on the bed again, and my toes start to uncurl. I feel drowsy with lust. That was so good and I don't even know how to tell Finn that. I don't know how to praise him because this is unlike anything I have ever experienced.

He sits up, wiping his mouth on his wrist before crawling on top of me. Anticipation starts in my spine, desperate for him to fill me. Everything so far has been so unbelievably good that I can't even fucking imagine how the sex is going to feel. I can't imagine how amazing it will be when he is finally inside of me.

"Good?" he asks, getting cocky. It's so funny to watch someone grow in front of your eyes. A few hours ago, we were sitting next to each other at the bar, and he was completely unsure of his performance in bed. Now, he has made me cum on his mouth in record time. I think I'm creating a monster.

"Ya think?" I say sarcastically, trying to be funny but it comes out more breathless and desperate than I intended. My entire body needs to feel him inside of me, to feel him fuck me finally.

"Do you have a condom?" he asks in between planting kisses on my neck. I blink a few times, trying to push the lust out of my brain and think for a second. If everything he did didn't feel so fucking good that would be easier.

"In the nightstand," I mutter, drunk on the feelings he gives me. I feel like we have been at this for days, but in reality, it has only been an hour at the most. Time feels like it goes faster when I am with Finn.

Finn leans over, finds a condom, and puts it on as fast as he can. His speed is once again impressive. His desperation to be inside of me is intoxicating.

"You ready?" he asks, eyes filled with fire. I nod curtly, desperate.

His cock enters me slowly, just like he has done with everything else. With how wet I already am, he slides in with ease, making my eyes roll into the back of my head. I adjust to his size as he enters, making me whimper. For some reason, I hoped his teasing would end here. I hoped he would fuck me like I need him to right away, but instead, he stares down at me, watching my reaction. His eyes grow darker the longer he teases me, the slower he goes. I'm so desperate for him to finally fuck me.

"Please?" I beg, unable to take anymore. My body is primed for him, ready. I have been so fucking desperate for so fucking long and I just need him to finish the job he started. I just need him to ruin me for everyone else. I just need him to claim my body as his own, finally giving me what I need.

My question flips a switch in Finn. He goes from slow and controlled to an animal fucking me for need more than for pleasure. He doesn't *want* to fuck me anymore, he *needs* it. He brings his body down on top of me, spreading my legs farther, allowing him to go deeper. His lips find mine, changing the tone in the air, making it more vulnerable. Our lips crash together as my hands dive into his hair, pulling him closer to me.

His cock thrusts into me in every way I have fucking needed. I have been waiting for this for the last few hours, imagining him fucking me hard enough to make my headboard smack into the wall. It feels like an out-of-body experience to finally be here. To finally be getting fucked the way I want.

"Holy fuck, Finn," I whisper in his ear, hoping he knows how fucking good this is for me. How fucking desperate I am to feel close to him. How much I don't want this to stop. Once it stops, the expectation is we go our separate ways, and I'm not ready to go there yet. I'm not ready to give this up.

"Yeah, say my fucking name," he groans into my ear, making pleasure run down my spine. "God, you are so fucking tight," he whispers again, making another orgasm build higher and higher in my body. His way with words is gonna be the thing to send me over the edge for the second time tonight.

He continues pounding into me, fucking me harder and harder the longer we go. The sound of our skin slapping together makes me delirious with pleasure. Every one of my senses is being toyed with and I can't fucking take it anymore.

His hand glides down, rubbing my clit similar to how he ate me out. He rubs in circles, exactly where I need him to.

"Finn—" I say, unable to finish my sentence because of how fucking good this feels.

"What, baby?" he asks, continuing to use my body how he sees fit. Suddenly my body is spasming around him, tightening around his cock. I moan louder, trying to show him that I am cumming, since I am unable to get the words out with the white hot pleasure coursing through my veins.

He keeps fucking me, only making it halfway through my orgasm before he falls over the cliff with me.

"Holy fucking—" he says, muffling his words with my hair. He buries his cock inside of me and his head in my shoulder, biting slightly. Not enough to hurt me, but enough to clue me in that he feels the same way I do.

I've never had sex like this. I have never been so pleased and vulnerable and bare and open all at once. I've never had this level of freedom with someone and I don't know how I am supposed to go back to mediocre sex with men who pretend to know what they are doing. Even the thought turns my stomach sour.

Chapter Eight

Finn

My breath comes out quickly as I do my best to catch it. That was like nothing I have experienced in my whole fucking life. I need to remember to send apology notes to the guys Emma has fucked before because I'm sorry they didn't get to experience what I just experienced. Everyone else in the world is missing out, and I think they should know.

I roll off of Emma, getting up quickly to dispose of the condom before returning. I'm not exactly sure what we are supposed to do now. Usually, with women, sex is a one-time thing. We both get what we want and then we move on. The problem is that I'm not so sure that's what I want right now. I don't want to just move on after this. This felt oddly bonding and I don't want to just walk away. I'm not sure how Emma feels, but I'm hoping she feels the same.

I lie down next to her, both of us still catching our breath. I lie on my side and prop my head on my elbow, just so I can stare at her for a few seconds. I reach out and move a few hairs out of her face, admiring her. She is just so fucking beautiful. Unlike anyone I have ever been around.

Her skin has a sheen to it, making her glow. Her red hair is a little bit of a mess, but in a I-just-got-fucked kind of way. Her brown eyes stare into mine, soaking in the moment.

"Do you feel like a new man?" Emma jokes, breaking the tension. I'm thankful she spoke first. I'm worried I'm going to say things that could freak her out. I'm worried she has different expectations for this than I do, and I'm going to be disappointed.

"Absolutely," I say with a smile, leaning in to give her a peck on the lips. I do it without thinking, pulling back after, and realizing maybe kissing is off the table now. "What do we do now?" I ask suddenly, needing answers to the questions filling my head.

"Well, I—" she starts, looking into my eyes like she has lost her voice. She closes her mouth and tries again. "What do you want to do?" she asks, breathlessly.

I give myself a second to think about her question. It feels weird to go into dating *after* having sex, but also I can't imagine walking away from this right now. I can't imagine walking away from someone I have opened up to so much. I can't imagine walking away from some I feel so comfortable opening up to like this.

"Do you want to grab coffee tomorrow?" I ask, hoping she feels the same way I do. I don't know the proper etiquette in times like this, but all I can do is be as truthful as possible and hope it doesn't kick me in the ass.

"I thought you'd never ask," she replies, a smile playing on her lips.

Epilogue

Emma

I try my best to smile and be polite to the man who has been talking to me for the last fifteen minutes, but it's hard when he keeps glancing down at my tits as if I don't notice. As if I'm not literally right here.

Finn warned me that this event was going to be pretty boring, but this takes the cake. Everyone comes up to talk to me, but only because they want to know the person who is on Finn's arm. All they do is brag to me about their money and it kind of disgusts me. I'm in a room full of people who could probably end world hunger and yet they are sitting in hundred-thousand-dollar dresses and suits discussing which yacht they should buy this summer because theirs is so outdated.

When the man in front of me looks at my tits for the fifth time in the last two minutes, I excuse myself. I don't care if it's rude anymore. It's rude to look at me like a piece of meat, but he doesn't seem to mind doing *that.*

I find Finn across the room and he is the only shining light in this awful place. He's talking to a couple of other guys, ones I have been told are "not that bad", but he ends the conversations quickly so they are gone by the time I make it over to him.

"These people are like vultures," I mutter when I'm finally close to him. I try to keep it quiet, not wanting to set off the one percent, but I have felt more like I'm at a zoo than a party with the way these people have been watching me.

"I saw the way William was looking at you," Finn mutters, clearly holding back anger. I glance up at him and smile, loving this side of him. "I'm going to have a word with him if he even glances at you again," he says, puffing out his chest.

"No, you won't," I whisper back, holding back a laugh.

"These people need to know that you are with me," he mutters, irritated.

"They know," I reassure lovingly.

Finn places a hand on my waist with a tight grip, and excitement quickly rushes through my body. I have watched Finn become more and more confident over the last few weeks, and it has been one of the hottest things I've ever seen. After a little bit of guidance, we both realized Finn likes to take the lead, he just needed a little help getting there.

A service I gladly supplied.

His hand moves to the small of my back, and shivers run down my spine, waiting for him to touch me more. I don't know if I will ever lose this feeling around him, feeling desperate for his touch.

"I wanna show you something," Finn whispers in my ear, leading me to the corners of the room which opens up to multiple hallways. I'm not sure exactly where we're going, but I know whatever he's planning to do to me is going to be hot, so I follow completely willingly, as he guides me by the hand.

I don't know my way around the building, but since Finn is technically one of the hosts, he has been here multiple times to help make choices for the event. He leads me around like he owns the place, commanding the room with his confidence.

We walk until we are in front of a set of stairs, and I glance at Finn with a question in my eyes. I assumed he would give me a hickey on the side of the room and that would be that, but stairs aren't needed for something so simple.

I watch as his arms move forward, motioning me down the stairs, and I take a deep breath before moving forward, descending into something that I'm sure will surprise me. Finn leads me down a hallway until he finds the door he's looking for, and leads me inside.

It's dark as fuck, and I can't make out a thing when the door slams. I jump at the noise, but Finn places a hand on my arm, comforting me instantly. The lights flick on and I give myself a second to adjust.

I'm in the last place I was expecting to be. I thought we would be going somewhere fancy, maybe a private room or at least someplace with a bed, but a broom closet was not on my list of possible destinations.

It's a small room, lined with metal shelves on the end holding supplies for cleaning the gala area. The walls are lined with brooms and mops, hung up only by small clips. The light above us flickers, which might make the room feel scary if I wasn't with Finn.

"Get on your knees," Finn says, breaking me out of my trance. My eyes shoot to his, trying to figure out if he is joking or not. His chest moves up and down quickly, as if he's worked up. I spare a glance down, noticing the thick bulge in his pants. My mouth waters in instinct, ready to taste him.

I move to my knees quickly, not questioning him for a second. He has slowly but surely become more demanding and I have been loving every second of it. Now that he knows how to work my body, he does it so confidently, as if his hands were made to use me.

"I'm going fuck the thought of any other man out of that pretty little head of yours," Finn says with a deep voice, sounding intimidating, but his eyes give him away. Although Finn is getting more and more confident in the way he talks in the bedroom, his eyes still hold a softness that calms me. Through everything, I know I'm in control. He does these things because I want him to, but he would stop at the drop of a hat if I reacted badly.

He holds love in his eyes and it calms my body's every cell. At least I hope it's love, because I know that's what I'm feeling for him.

He works on the button of his pants slowly, making the anticipation build within me. I can feel my body reacting to him already, and he hasn't even taken his cock out yet. My nipples are tight and sensitive and I keep rubbing my thighs together, just a little, to attempt some level of friction.

"God, you make my cock so fucking hard," Finn grunts out, making my mouth water for what's to come, or should I say what's to cum. Head was never a favorite activity of mine, but god, with Finn? I could do it all fucking day. The way he talks to me while I suck him off is something made of dreams. I have never felt so good while gagging on a dick before.

He pushes his pants down, finally revealing the bulge he's sporting. God, I can't fucking wait. His underwear goes next, finally allowing me to see the thick cock that Finn is going to shove down my throat. I could cum at the thought alone.

"Open your fucking mouth," Finn grits out through clenched teeth. I can hear how badly he wants this, just based on the voice he uses. I've gotten to know almost every voice he has, each one seemingly better than the next.

Once again, his words come off as demanding but his eyes hold a lightness that keeps me grounded. He watches for signs that I'm uncomfortable, trying to uncover signals that I am enjoying myself without forcing me to open my mouth and utter those words to him.

That's probably my favorite thing about being with Finn. He is always trying to anticipate my needs for me, so I don't have to tell him. Of course, sometimes I hide it better than he can see it, but he is getting better and better at reading me.

I open my mouth for him instantly, ready to feel his cock touch my tongue. He acts instantly, excitement showing on his face and throughout his body. His thighs are tight, showing all of the muscle sitting there, ready for me to feel with my hands. He looks tense, but in the best kind of way.

The tip of his cock touches my tongue and I can't hold back the groan from escaping my mouth. I have become a cock sucking enthusiast since meeting Finn.

"Yeah, you fucking like that don't you?" Finn mutters before sliding his cock deeper into my mouth. I can feel my panties start to get wet, but I ignore the urge to touch myself. I'm too focused on the dick sitting in my mouth and the man in need of a release.

I suck slowly as he lightly fucks my mouth, only bringing his dick in and out an inch or two to start, allowing me time to prep before I take the entire thing. I press my thighs together, desperate for friction, and I see the glint in Finn's eyes when he notices how badly turned on I am.

"Be a good girl and touch yourself, baby" Finn says, staring me in the eyes. We've done this before, at home, but never in a fucking supply closet. The idea of it thrills me more than I expected it would.

I slide my hand down my body slowly, making Finn suffer. He tracks my hand with his eyes, watching with greed as I get closer and closer to touching myself. Finn groans when I finally reach the edge of my dress, making my clit pulse with need. God, this is so fucking hot.

Finn is still sliding his cock in and out of my mouth, but the closer I get to touching myself, the more force he puts behind his thrusts. I have never had much of a gag reflex, but with the size of Finn, he pushes me to the max.

I slide my hands into the seam of my panties, making my nipples harden with desire. I reach my other hand up, squeezing my nipple in between my fingers. Without even thinking, I groan with pleasure, desperate to get off with Finn staring at me the way he is.

"Holy shit, yeah baby. Make yourself cum while my cock is in your whore mouth," Finn says, continuing to stare at me with lust filling his eyes. God, he has gotten so fucking good at dirty talk. I could cum from his words alone. I groan as I start rubbing circles with my hand, and this is the moment Finn decides to shove his entire cock down my throat. I suppress a gag as he drags it out slowly, still staring at my every movement.

His body is controlled, and if I didn't know him as well as I do, I wouldn't be able to tell that the slight shake of his legs means he's getting close. He is always so controlled, but the second he starts getting close to cumming, his body shows it.

I add to the pressure with my mouth, sucking harder than before, loving the sounds coming out of him when I do. He groans loudly. I would be worried about people hearing if I gave a fuck at this point. My only focus is the beautiful man in front of me who is about to cum in my mouth.

I feel so fucking sensitive. My hand is working my clit like a pro, and my eyes keep trying to roll to the back of my head. I keep them on Finn, not wanting to miss a minute of him coming apart, but it's hard. I can feel my orgasm building quickly. I'm not sure if it's the thrill of doing this in a public-ish place or just the fact that I find everything Finn does insanely sexy.

"Holy fuck, Finn..." I say, not finishing my sentence. He knows what I'm about to say. He knows how close I am to cumming while sitting on the floor of a supply closet with his cock in my mouth.

"Say it," Finn demands, looking me dead in the eyes. His brown eyes are darker than normal, getting closer to black the closer I get to my orgasm. "Don't you dare fucking cum before you say it," Finn adds, making my orgasm start to teeter over the edge.

"Holy fuck, I'm going to cum, baby," I moan, before he shoves his cock down my throat, quieting my moans. I finally close my eyes as my orgasm takes over. The added sensation of Finn fucking my face only adds to the pleasure coursing through my veins. I keep my fingers on my clit, rubbing circles to ride out the high.

When I finally come down and open my eyes, Finn is standing above me, barely hanging on.

"That was the hottest fucking thing I've ever seen," Finn grunts out, barely hanging on. He keeps fucking my mouth, his cock sliding deeper and deeper until my gag reflex starts to feel it. I choke it down, sucking and gagging, but taking it.

"God, you are so good at taking it, you know that?" Finn asks, making my thighs clench together. If I thought he could hang on longer, I would try to cum again.

His cock leaves my mouth for a second, giving me a second to breathe and tell Finn exactly what I want. "Cum in my throat," I mutter, desperate. I have never been a fan of swallowing, but watching the way Finn's face lights up with lust, I would do anything for him.

His eyes darken and his body takes a more dominant stance. I open my mouth again, willing him inside. Waiting for him to fill my throat with his cum.

He complies instantly, taking my mouth as his, and literally fucking any thoughts out of it. Not just thoughts of men, but thoughts of anything. The only thing on my mind is the way his cock slides against my tongue every time he enters, making me rub my thighs together. I can only think about the way he hits the back of my throat, and then goes a little deeper, making my eyes fill with tears.

The only thing filling my mind is thoughts of the man that I have fallen in love with over the last few weeks.

A groan alerts me before his cum starts leaking into my mouth. I swallow as it comes, mainly focused on the groans coming out of his mouth. I could do this every day when he makes sounds like this.

I swallow one last time, before popping his cock out of my mouth with one final suck, and stare into his eyes for a second. Finn chuckles a little, still coming down from his orgasm, but his eyes hold such love that it fills my heart completely. He pulls his pants up quickly, making us both ready to resume the party as if nothing happened.

He helps me to my feet before planting a kiss on my lips. I smile into the kiss, happy he would rather kiss me than give a shit about what I just swallowed.

He pulls away, only an inch, leaving our foreheads still connected. "God, I'm gonna fucking marry you someday, you know that?" Finn says, staring into my eyes, into my soul.

I smile back at him, knowing I can't fucking wait for that day.

Books By This Author

Taught Right (She Teaches Him #2):

What happens when Joey, who just wants to be taught right, hires Ava, who knows exactly how to teach him?

F*cked Right (She Teaches Him #3):

What happens when Jace, who has never done this before, gets f*cked right by Callie, who knows exactly what she's doing?

Greedy:

What happens when the best kind of revenge, is fucking your ex-boyfriend's business rival?

About The Author

Rhianna Burwell is an Amazon best seller in erotica. Author of the Before series and the She Teaches Him series, available on Kindle Unlimited, she takes pride in writing spicy, realistic, and deeply satisfying romance and erotica. Rhianna currently resides in Minnesota, where—when she's not writing erotica hot enough to melt all the winter snows—she enjoys curling up with her cat, avidly watching Grey's Anatomy, and reading—her current fav is alien romance. Rhianna loves to hear from readers, who can connect with via any of her social media links.

Instagram: @rhiannaburwellauthor

Tiktok: @rhiannaburwellauthor

Printed in Great Britain
by Amazon

29571695R00051